*In memory of
the incomparable
Sam Rodia
(1879-1965)*

ALLEN A. KNOLL, PUBLISHERS

NICE TO SEE

ILLUSTRATED BY PETER HAMLIN

STORY BY THEODORE ROOSEVELT GARDNER

Publisher's Cataloging in Publication

Gardner, Theodore Roosevelt.
    Something nice to see / Theodore Roosevelt Gardner II, ;
  illustrations by Peter Hamlin.
    p. cm.
    SUMMARY: When Barry, a boy living in Watts, is rejected by his
  classmates because he can read, he is comforted by Sam, an Italian
  immigrant who is also different. Story in verse features the
  builder of Watts Towers, Sam Rodia.
    Preassigned LCCN: 93-61121.
    ISBN 0-9627297-6-0

    1. Rodia, Simon, 1879-1965--Juvenile fiction. 2. Simon Rodia's
  Towers (Watts, Los Angeles, Calif.)--Juvenile fiction. 3.
  [Self-acceptance--Fiction. 4. Stories in rhyme.] I. Hamlin,
  Peter, ill. II. Title.

  PZ8.3.G37 1993   [Fic]
                       QBI93-21682

Printed and Bound by Horowitz/Rae Book Manufacturers, Inc., New York.
Color separations by Photolith Systems, Santa Barbara, Ca.

In the small town of Watts lived a boy named Barry.
His mom said he was getting too big to carry.
So she taught him to multiply, to eighty-one,
He learned letters too, he thought it was fun.

Barry's father left home some years before,
His mother said they would see him no more.
There was more work without her man,
So Barry said, "I'll help if I can."

Barry's mom brought him up in the neighborhood
And taught him to be the good boy he should.
She taught him to read and taught him to write
And taught him too, it was bad to fight.

Across Barry's street in a triangle space
Stood a house and yard, not commonplace.
Dancing there was a funny little fellow
Whose back was as stiff as a very old cello.

Now the man Barry saw was five feet tall,
Which isn't tall for a man at all.
He was a shy guy with the slightest frame,
So quiet, few knew Sam was his name.

He wore torn pants and a very old shirt,
And both were covered with lots of dirt.
Sam came from Italy, a far-off spot,
His English, he said, was not so hot.

Sam lived next door to a railroad track;
He could see the trains from his yard in back.
When the trains were gone he collected things
Like bottles and plates and even bedsprings.

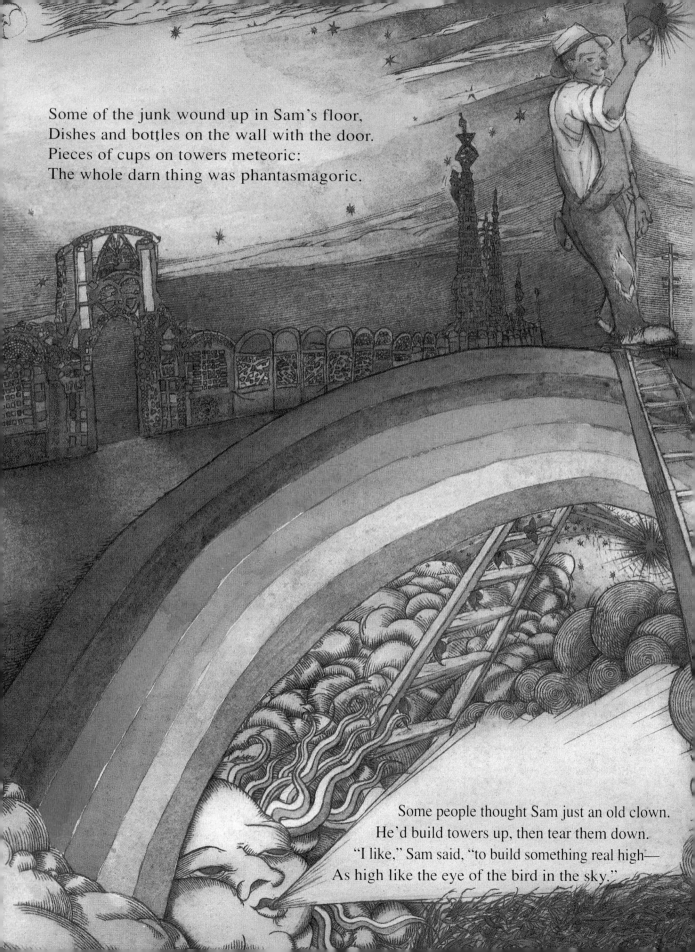

Some of the junk wound up in Sam's floor,
Dishes and bottles on the wall with the door.
Pieces of cups on towers meteoric:
The whole darn thing was phantasmagoric.

Some people thought Sam just an old clown.
He'd build towers up, then tear them down.
"I like," Sam said, "to build something real high—
As high like the eye of the bird in the sky."

For days Barry silently watched the man build
And wondered how soon his yard would be filled.
For there were walls and walkways and towers
Made of pieces of dishes like flowers.

"Well, young fella, is good what you see,
This things I am do for you and for me?"
It was Sam who broke the silence at last,
And Barry's shyness disappeared so fast.

"My name is Barry and I can read."
"Well," said Sam, "well, well, yes indeed!
For a boy small as you, is a good start.
I think you young boy, you be very smart."

"And tomorrow," said Barry, "I go to school."
"Ah yes," Sam said. "That good as a rule.
If you want to be smarter than a weed
Much better for you to learn to read."

The school teacher asked, "Who can read books?"
"I can," Barry said with the slyest of looks.
And he read his first day, the best he could—
His teacher smiled and said, "That's good."

But on the playground at recess
Barry had much less success.
When the girls looked at Barry they giggled
And twisted and turned and hiccuped and wiggled.

"We don't want to play or stay with you,
So go away, find something else to do."
When Barry came near, the angry boys parted
And called him names (he was so broken-hearted).

His mom tried to tell him how jealous folks got
When you could do something they could not.
He didn't understand why that should be.
"They can learn to read," he said, "just like me."

He told this to Sam who was working away
On his towers, stretching the light of day.
"I have my dreams, that nice for me;
So I build something nice to see.

"Many peoples they be cruel to me too,
'Cause I immigrant and no talk like you.
People who be nasty to people is wrong—
And this it go on much too long."

When Sam completed his little tile ship,
He said to the boy, "Wanna take a trip?
Dream tonight, when you finally snooze,
You take my boat for a big long cruise."

That night in his bed, Barry shut his eyes
And closed out the dark, the hate and the lies.
He started to think of Sam's seashell ship
And what the ship would be like for a trip.

There in his vision, the boat stood quite tall,
With tile and seashells—a bright music hall.
With layers of stuff and three tiers in the middle,
And five tall masts, one bowed like a fiddle.

Barry had, on his ship, a friendly crew
Of people he liked, who liked him too.
The boat was big and strong on the waves,
And Barry sailed it to an island with caves.

The magic began when the ship touched shore,
Here he was happy with friends galore.
The seashells and tile on Sam's ship came alive
And flew to the shore like bees to a hive.

In this special land there was much to do
And so many friends who said, "We like you."
There was a castle like Sam's Watts towers,
Where Barry and friends read books for hours.

Barry smiled at Sam the next day,
Sam smiled too, "You been away?
I see you learn to dream great stuff,
Life for you won't be so tough.

"But always remember, Barry, in the end,
You should always be your own best friend.
You don't got to be like other boys are:
Do what you like and you be a star.

"My towers they finished," said Sam one day,
"I am go North, I go on my way.
I made my dream for all to see;
You my good friend, so take my key."

"But, Sam," said Barry, "you can't leave town,
Your beautiful work deserves great renown."
"Famous," said Sam, "mean nothing to me—
I have finally make something nice to see.

"My work it is done, it's 30-some years;
It was fun while it lasts, but now no tears!
Fame or fortune is not my survival,
My joy's in the journey, not the arrival."